THE DUE SEASON

Matt Hilton

Matt Hilton Books

Copyright © 2019/2024 Matthew Hilton

Cover image used under a standard content license from
WWW.PIXABAY.COM/Reznik89

All rights reserved

The characters and events portrayed in this book are fictitious. Any similarity to real persons, living or dead, is coincidental and not intended by the author.

No part of this book may be reproduced, or stored in a retrieval system, or transmitted in any form or by any means, electronic, mechanical, photocopying, recording, or otherwise, without express written permission of the publisher.

CONTENTS

Title Page
Copyright
Foreword
THE DUE SEASON   1
Acknowledgement   35
About The Author   37

FOREWORD

This short story sits within the universe I created wherein my protagonist Joe Hunter, and his best friend and business partner, Jared "Rink" Rington, exist. The Due Season features two of Hunter's most despicable enemies, both on a collision course to meet each other in a kill or be killed contest. It is a battle of knife versus garotte, and many other killing weapons beside, to find out who is the baddest of the bad.

This story takes place somewhere/time between Dead Men's Harvest (Joe Hunter #6) and The Fourth Option (Joe Hunter #13).

Enjoy,
Matt Hilton

THE DUE SEASON

by Matt Hilton

Kitty Hawk Bay, Barrier Islands, North Carolina

'Why are you doing this, Marty?'

'Shhh. I'm busy.'

'Please…don't.'

Marty held up a finger glistening with blood. 'A moment's hush, if you will. Then I'll get back to you.'

Catherine Bryant's eyelids scrunched, but there was no escaping the horrendous sound. She moaned in horror.

The wet rasping halted, replaced by Marty's hollow footsteps. He came to rest a few feet from her, and she heard him humming in contemplation. 'Um, yeah,' he decided. 'This is a nice piece. Whaddaya reckon, Doc? One for the trinket cabinet?'

She averted her face, twisting with revulsion.

'Aw, c'mon, we both know you ain't the squeamish type.'

Catherine whispered a prayer under her breath.

Marty touched her cheek. His fingertip was tacky. Catherine cringed, squeezed her eyelids tighter. Something warmer and harder than his finger tapped her on the forehead. 'C'mon, one little look won't hurt you.'

'Please don't…'

Marty puffed in exasperation. 'This is on you, Doc. You knew the consequences.'

'But…but I've only ever tried to help you.'

'And I shall be eternally grateful. But it doesn't change the deal we made, Doc.' His thumb and forefinger pinched her cheeks together, forcing her to pout. He touched his prize to her bottom lip, and she reared back to escape. Her bindings, and the metal chair she was tied to, resisted her. His thumb and finger dug deeper, working to prise open her jaw. She clenched her teeth, but the force exerted on the cluster of nerve endings beneath her cheekbones made her gasp. Marty inserted the tip of his prize. Catherine spat and squirmed to expel it.

'First you act squeamish, and now coy! Go on Doc, just give it a little suck.' He laughed though, and walked away. Catherine peered through slitted lids at him. He still limped slightly, and held his right elbow clenched to his side. Otherwise he had regained most of his mobility. In the months he'd been her patient, his bodily injuries had largely healed, but alas there was nothing she could do for his psychopathy. It had been evident right from the beginning, and there was nothing she could do to change him: in return for making him well again he'd promised he wouldn't slay her entire family. If she told *anyone* about him, he'd warned, there'd be no mercy. Never had she believed his threat was a bluff.

He crouched, his right leg held stiff to one side. Began undoing shirt buttons.

'Marty,' she pleaded, 'think about what you're doing. This has to stop.'

Without halting his task he looked over his shoulder at her. Before suturing his head wound she'd shaved his hair. It had regrown, but the thick scar tissue extending from his forehead to the top of his cranium would never regain growth. Another purple scar slashed across his jawline from beneath the lobe of his right ear to his chin; on that side she'd removed broken teeth and fixed the sundered mandible. Despite the horrendous scars, they framed an almost boyish face, and eyes into which even she — a woman old enough to be his mother — had fallen more than once.

'I tried stopping. But you started me again.' He smiled, only one side of his mouth rising. 'You should have kept to our deal, Doc, and I'd have kept to mine.'

'I did nothing wrong! I never called the cops!'

'But you let them in the house. If only you'd sent them away, this wouldn't have happened.' He returned to his task, grunting at the effort as he stripped the uniform shirt off Sheriff's Deputy Mike Buford's corpse.

Catherine tried not to look at the dead

lawman's face; she'd known him since he was a boy when she'd treated his chickenpox. Before retiring from her country practise, she'd also treated Buford's children's ailments too.

Marty stood from him, holding up the shirt and checking it against the light streaming in through a window. There was a small dark patch on the collar, but surprisingly little other blood had leaked from the wound where Marty had driven a meat skewer through his ear canal into his brain. The second man lying at the threshold of her kitchen was bloodier. Without a care to salvage his voluminous uniform shirt, Marty had gone at the overweight deputy, Bobby Grainger, with a knife from her meat block. He'd stabbed repeatedly with such force most of Grainger's ribs were broken, and his lungs were blood-filled sacks. His forearm was laid open like a filleted fish. It was from him that Marty had sawn a three-inch chunk of ulna bone, and from which he'd tried to have her suck the blood.

'Please don't go after my family,' Catherine croaked.

'I must. What kind of man would I be if I didn't keep my word?' Marty stripped out of his own blood-splashed shirt. His body was pale and gaunt: his skin hadn't seen sunlight since he'd washed up on a nearby beach months ago, and Catherine, retired from practise though she was, had been summoned to save his life. It was while she'd transported him in her car, mumbling in delirium from his bullet and knife injuries and a subsequent immersion in a storm-racked sea, that he'd sat up and devilish promise had shone from his eyes. He'd offered his one-sided deal and instead of to the hospital she'd taken him home.

How Catherine now wished that she'd smothered him in his sleep that first day. The Hippocratic oath she'd sworn was not what had stayed her, but genuine terror that he might wake and stop her. She doubted that even having been shot, stabbed and hacked - one bullet having glanced from his skull and pitched him from the deck of a ship – he wouldn't possess the strength to murder a frail elderly lady. His survival instinct went beyond anyone's she'd come across before, and it was only overshadowed by his desire to take life.

'You don't have to harm them,' she pleaded, thinking of her twin daughters and six grandchildren. 'I know you won't let me live, but put an end to the killing here. Only you and I know what was agreed…God! Please don't hurt my babies!'

He moved towards her, his game leg hitching with each step. The deputy's shirt hung loose on his spare frame. 'Now you want to revise the terms of our agreement, Doc? What can you do for me that I can't do for myself? What exactly can you offer in return for their lives?'

She had no bargaining power.

Marty suddenly halted. He laid the chunk of bone on his forearm, juxtaposing it alongside his recently healed ulna. He thought, all the while probing his tongue across the shards of broken molars and the uneven surface of his cheek. He looked up, and again one side of his mouth pulled up in a smile. 'There's one thing you can offer me. Do so willingly and I promise to leave your brats be.'

'Will...will you kill me first?'

'Of course, Doc. You've been good to me, and I'm not a total bastard, so I'll do the right thing and put you out of your misery first.' He shoved away the bone in his jeans pocket, replacing it with the surgical bone saw he'd tucked in his belt after mutilating Deputy Grainger. 'Besides, I can't have you screaming the entire time. Being a surgeon you must know that excising a jawbone requires some precise and excruciatingly painful cuts.'

Tuscarora Lake, Minnesota

Almost as far north as he could drive before he'd have to switch to an ATV to negotiate the boggy terrain, Marty fetched up at a hunter's cabin only a few miles short of the Canadian border. He was in a wedge of Minnesota known as the Land of Ten Thousand Lakes near the western shore of Lake Superior. It had never been his plan to head to this wilderness, but it was as good as anywhere to hide from his pursuers. Without a doubt, the slayings at Doctor Bryant's house bore his trademarked style and would have set off alarm klaxons. Though his identity would have been kept secret from law enforcement, even from the feds, a certain black budget agency would have set hounds on his trail.

Disguised in the liberated uniform, he'd driven the deputies' cruiser off the Barrier Islands into North Carolina proper. There he'd pulled over another motorist, then left the young guy's corpse seated in the patrol car, now wearing Deputy Buford's shirt but missing the index finger from his right hand. Marty drove south, ditched the young man's car on the outskirts of Savannah, Georgia, and then liberated another vehicle and another index finger from a young woman ending a hard day's work as a waitress at a roadside diner. His journey took him across country, and he didn't slow until Talladega, where he abandoned his latest ride and hailed a cab into Birmingham, Alabama. Over the next two days he purchased bus and train tickets to a number of destinations as far flung as Texas and Florida, all under the watchful gaze of CCTV at the bus and train stations. Of all of those tickets, he used only one, boarding a bus to St. Louis but hopped off again at its first scheduled stop at Tupelo, from where he hitched a ride north. In Corinth, he denied the urge to slay his driver, and instead hitched another ride, this time into Arkansas. Once there, he rested up, but behaved, and again thumbed a ride, heading back east all the way to Atlanta with a couple of born again hippies who took pity on his disfigurement and crippled body. They were awfully surprised when his gimpy leg and atrophied arm proved no impediments to murder when he gutted them both in the rear of their camper van. He took care to burn the van, and any forensic evidence inside it, and again denied the urge to take a trophy from each corpse: the hippies had died for the simple reason his wounded face was too distinctive to forget and he'd already gone to so much trouble to lay a false trail for them to later identify his movements to his inevitable hunters. Let some other killer take the props for their slaying, he decided, and the heat off his back.

His path led through many states, and now and again, he did take another trophy, but never when it would indicate where he'd travelled next. It took him two months to wend his way to the shores of Tuscarora Lake, and by then he was reasonably confident he'd left Arrowsake's bloodhounds sniffing cold trails and scratching their heads somewhere in the Deep South. Being constantly on the move could be wearing on a traveller, but he'd thrived. His thigh wound barely troubled him anymore, and much of the muscle tone had been regained in his damaged arm. Even his fair hair had grown in, and he found he liked his new locks — for years since his stint with the Secret Service he'd always favoured a short, neat preppy style — because it helped disguise the furrow cut into his scalp by his would-be executioner's final bullet. It also matched the bohemian clothing he'd recently affected, and helped him blend in with other tow-headed off-gridders frequenting the district.

Out of season, the hunting cabin was

deserted, but as was the way with other cabins he'd come across in his previous wanderings it was stocked with the essentials of food and firewood. It was an unwritten rule with some outdoorsmen and women that they left their cabins ready for habitation on their return, or should it be needed by somebody in dire need of shelter: reciprocation was the key, where anyone using their facilities should ensure they replenished the provisions for the next person who might need them. Marty made use of some tinned goods from the larder, and then neatly arranged his collection of bones on the shelf. Of course, he'd no intention that they'd ever become the stock for a pan of heart-warming soup.

He couldn't stay indefinitely, but for now the hunting cabin was home. Being transient by nature the concept of home was a strange one to Marty. Perhaps it was due to his extended stay in the care of the good Doctor Bryant that he'd grown too comfortable between her walls, and now longed for the permanency of a place of his own, but that could never be. If he put down roots anywhere his pursuers would find him. Besides, sooner or later, the owners of the cabin would show up, and there'd only be one outcome if they tried to evict him, and that would ensure a visit from Arrowsake: Walter Hayes Conrad was a dogged foe and his bloodhounds some of the most tenacious he'd ever met.

The third time's the charm, he'd heard said. Well, twice already he'd survived battle royals with Conrad's most determined pet slayer: though not as the winner in either match. If the universe cared at all, then Marty was due a triumph, except he knew the universe was a chaotic beast and couldn't give a damn for the dramas of men. Marty once believed that he was a Prince of Chaos, but he was kidding himself. By the nature of the beast the self-imposed title was a contradiction. He could act chaotic when it came to the disregard of men's laws, but if he hoped for victory in the end game, he'd better have all of his ducks in a row.

Vince Everett was a legend. Not in the context of fame or historical acts, but in the sense that Everett was the cloak worn to disguise an assassin's identity. The original Everett was an abusive racist hillbilly who swaggered through life, oiling his ducktails and doling out extreme violence at a whim, and who'd died ingloriously with a dirty needle stuck in his arm. The persona was one that Stephen Vincent could affect at the flick of his pompadour, and one he'd worn on numerous occasions to good effect. Super assassins weren't all slick dudes in tuxedoes and driving sports cars, some were as brash as they came and Vince Everett was as subtle as a running kick to the balls. He wasn't in to the subtleties of polonium poisoning, or even using a sniper rifle from half a mile distant, he preferred his kills to be up close and personal, his victims throttled with a guitar string so he could watch the veins explode in their eyes and their tongues loll from their gaping mouths. The trouble was, his target was equally dangerous, and also preferred his kills to be so close they were intimate.

For that matter, Vince brought friends to the fight. If Vince couldn't best him in mano-a-mano combat, he'd have his buddies hold the bastard still while he sawed off his head with his G-string garrotte.

Including Vince, there was four of them altogether, each highly trained and highly motivated. They were unlike the Arrowsake of old — soldiers gleaned from the cream of Special Forces — because these men had no compunction about cold-blooded murder for murder's sake: if they weren't sanctioned by the highest of powers they'd be no less murderous psychopaths than those they hunted. They were each deniable operators of the darkest calibre, wet work aficionados, tasked with delivering the head of Martin Maxwell to Walter Conrad. Once Conrad had hoped to recruit Maxwell to his mission, but there was no safe way of controlling a bone harvesting serial killer, which Conrad had learned to his disappointment, and the slaughter of too many innocent souls. If the higher powers to which Conrad answered learned that his pet project had survived his battle on the high seas, the scandal could prove too enormous to escape, and it would be his ruination. As far as ultra secret black-ops went, only Conrad, and not the cabal of grey men and women who'd be his masters, sanctioned this hit. Ergo, they moved on the hunting cabin sans the assistance of technology, resources and high tech armament of the intelligence community behind them. Had they worked under the auspices of officialdom, once they'd identified Maxwell was home, they could have ordered in a drone strike and bombed the shit out of him. But it suited all, because without exception, each was a warrior that favoured blades and bullets, blood and snot and their enemy's severed head at their feet.

The cabin was nestled at the edge of a mound crowned by low, stunted trees. On all sides the terrain was a network of bogs dotted with small similarly crowned islands and wider expanses of open water. To the unwary the land between the islands looked negotiable, but mostly the tall grasses grew from a mat of decomposing roots, with sucking mud beneath. Even the hardiest of off-road vehicles could easily be mired if they strayed from the well worn paths…walking in could be equally tricky for most, but there were few options for Vince and his fellow killers. Driving in, their target would be alerted to their approach long before they were ready to face him.

When he wasn't stalking man, there was nothing more that Ronnie Dietz enjoyed than tracking and bringing down game with a bow. He was an experienced woodsman, and didn't view the terrain as an obstacle. Therefore, he led the other two killers to individual observation points, hundreds of yards out, where for three nights they scoped the cabin, surveilling Maxwell's movements and relaying them back via a dedicated radio channel to Vince. They each had the opportunity to take out their target with a long range shot, but neither took it: Vince wouldn't tolerate a miss where Maxwell might flee and extend their hunt for another six darn months. Vince was waiting for the new moon, when the night would be at its darkest; then, and only then, would the quartet move in and execute him.

From their hides Cal Gerard and Parker Simmons endured the swarming bugs, the mud and discomfort, lying on tarps on the cold earth in rubber boots and Ghillie suits, as they watched Maxwell through their infra-red scopes. Meanwhile, Vince and Dietz prepped to storm the cabin. Two days of inactivity would have had a detrimental effect on Gerard's and Simmons' mental and physical beings, their minds would be dulled and their muscles less supple than usual, both conditions that could effect their reaction time: even a split-second's delay could prove the death of either of them. Therefore Vince and Dietz must be at the pinnacle of their game, and be the ones to make the initial incursion while their friends covered them.

A storm howling down from Canada conspired against Maxwell on the third night. The ink black sky and the roaring wind both concealed his hunters' approach and the faint noises they made. Vince waited until after Maxwell doused the lamp in his bedroom, then gave him an extra half hour to drift off to sleep before ordering the others to move in. While Gerard and Simmons shambled in through the sucking mud from opposites sides of the island, Dietz came from the north, following a well-worn game trail. Vince braved a gun shot by treading the road down which Maxwell had originally approached his temporary hideout. He was confident that he wouldn't be shot, because though he was no stranger to guns, Maxwell was a knifeman to his core. Vince held a prepped Beretta down by his thigh. He wasn't averse to shooting, but the pistol was a back-up weapon: his coiled garrotte would be the end of Maxwell. The others were armed, but with express orders to shoot to wound only, Vince wanted Maxwell conscious when the guitar string dropped over his head and cinched around his throat.

Parker Simmons moved carefully. He was still sheathed in the formless Ghillie suit, an extra layer of local grass and reeds woven into it for perfect camouflage. Every few yards of progress he halted, hunkering down in the muck, looking exactly like any of the other dozens of hummocks of higher ground in the bog. He'd listen and observe for a long beat, then only move on when he was certain he hadn't been spotted. On the far side of the island, his buddy Gerard would be following a similar approach pattern. They had timed their advance so they converged on the island at the same time as Dietz arrived from the north, Vince from the south, cutting off all possible avenues of escape.

Simmons cradled a rifle, but would only employ its firepower as a last resort. Occasionally he raised its scope to his eye and made a closer inspection of the cabin. Inside he watched a dim glow flicker to life behind the shuttered bedroom window. Maxwell was up and about: perhaps he'd risen from his bed to take a piss. Simmons envied him; his bladder was fit to bursting point but he'd missed the opportunity to empty it before Vince ordered the advance. He triple-clicked his radio — a prearranged signal — to alert the others of movement, and received clicks from each in response.

Ten feet closer he hunkered down again, matting his silhouette in against a tall stand of reeds, and once more scoped the cabin. The light went off. He double-clicked the all-clear signal, just as rain battered him. He swore under his breath.

'Hell of a night to be out on, eh?' whispered a voice from the night.

His reaction was his undoing. Simmons looked for the source of the voice before bringing around his rifle, and then it was too late.

From the tall reeds beside him a figure coated in black mud and grass had risen; Maxwell didn't dally when it came to employing his weapon. A broad-bladed knife fixed to a pole with duct tape speared through Simmons' Ghillie, plunging into his mouth that had opened in surprise. The tip of the blade scraped on the inner curve of his skull as Maxwell gave it a twist to scramble his would-be captor's brain. When Simmons sank down in death, his killer followed suit, and again both made formless shapes in the night.

Ronnie Dietz advanced with his bow nocked. Under ordinary circumstances he could put an arrow through the ace on a playing card at two hundred paces, or preferably through a man's eye socket. The storm though would affect his shot, with the wind and rain cutting almost sideways through the woods. The act of nature was a boon under which to spring a trap, but it also had its disadvantages. Vince had stalled too long in allowing Maxwell to settle down like that, and now they'd the damn storm to contend with instead of having things over and done with before it arrived in all its fury. Rain drummed on his shoulders, pattered from the bill of his cap, and the sound almost drowned the triple-click alarm through his earpiece. From his position, he couldn't yet see the cabin, let alone the light that briefly came on, only to be extinguished again shortly after. But he paused, waiting for the all-clear signal, and it came. He advanced, one foot in front of the other, his recurved bow poised to drive an arrow through Maxwell at any instant.

Overhead the tops of the trees thrashed in the storm. Small twigs and leaves rained. The incessant wind dirged; the moaning of a dying behemoth. All were distractions if he'd allow them places in his mind. Instead he concentrated on his footing.

An unwary man would have walked directly

into the open jaws of the steel trap. It had been laid on the game trail, camouflaged beneath a layer of broken twigs and tufts of moss plucked from the nearest tree trunks. Perhaps a dumb animal wouldn't have noted the stripped moss, or even the retaining chain driven into the ground by a spike, but the trap was obvious to him. He shook his head at its ineptness, and moved off the trail, lowering his bow and squeezing between the boles of two trunks to bypass the illegal bear trap. Where there was one trap on the game trail, there could be others, but he wasn't about to tread in any of them.

He felt the snag across his upper chest as he cleared the two trees, and realized his mistake.

While he avoided the steel teeth on the ground, he'd missed the trip wire across his new path. It was on a hair trigger, the thin wire coiling away as it sprung. Erupting from the grass underfoot, a wire snare yanked tightly around his knees. Dietz stumbled momentarily, but caught himself. The snare was designed to trap smaller game than a guy weighing one hundred and ninety-five pounds. He grunted in annoyance, released his hold on his arrow to give the wire a tug to yank it free of its mooring: and understood instantly that the chest high snag hadn't been set to catch a rabbit. Yanking the snare released a second trigger, and encumbered by the wire around his knees there was no avoiding the dead fall that thundered down on him from above. The sawn log was equal to his weight, but spearing down its more compact shape crushed him, and beat him to the earth.

Cal Gerard heard the crashing of falling branches. For the first time since they'd advanced he was pleased he was wading through mud on open ground, rather than traversing the woods like Dietz. In this storm the branches must be raining like confetti at a Vegas wedding. He'd grown up in the woods alongside the Appalachian Trail and knew to keep out of the forest when the hardest winds blew: he knew of two victims from his town who'd been crushed by aptly named Widow Makers, when the rotted tops of trees gave up the fight and submitted to gravity. He wouldn't like to be on the receiving end of a toppling tree or broken branch. The first man he'd known crushed had died instantly; the second hadn't been as fortunate: he'd spent the rest of his agonized life in a wheel chair, drooling soup down his shirtfront and crapping in man-sized diapers.

Had he also heard a cry?

Was Dietz hurt?

He clicked his radio.

In response he received three separate clicks in sequence as his compatriots checked in.

He moved forward. Off to his left he caught movement in the darkness, Vince approaching from the front of the house. He was indistinct in the gloom, his upper torso bent forward against the wind as he stalked towards the front door. The cabin blocked any view of Simmons, and Dietz was still under cover of the woods: he had no idea how ironic his latter thought was.

Gerard took another step and felt the ground slip away under him. He dug in with his heels, casting around for stability, but only sunk deeper, as a slope under his rubber boots pitched him deeper into a trough. Only then did he notice the disturbances in the grasses around him, realising that they had been cut and then re-laid to cover a deep trench excavated at the edge of the bog. He was being drawn down into a clenching embrace of soupy mud and dirty water. To save his life, he threw his weight forward clawing for stable ground, and lost his gun. There was no stable ground and the water invading his chest-high waders and Ghillie suit pulled him deeper. In a mild panic he fought to free his torso of the clinging netting, and only helped force him deeper into the quagmire. He fought with the shoulder straps holding his waders in place, trying to squirm free. He swallowed brackish water, spluttering and coughing, and would have yelled for assistance if it wouldn't compromise the mission.

Fuck the mission, he was drowning!

He opened his mouth to yell, but was swamped and went beneath the surface. Cut divots of reeds swarmed in overhead.

A hundred yards distant, his team leader crouched, watching as one of his men succumbed to a trap laid by one who was expecting them.

Vince Everett knew they'd supremely underrated the survival instincts of one who'd made his existence one of murder and living to reap in the afterglow his trophies brought him. Martin Maxwell had gone to ground at the hunting cabin, but he hadn't been idle during the weeks it'd taken to hunt him to this outpost in the Land of Ten Thousand Lakes. He'd prepared for when his hunters came for him, digging trenches in the boggy surroundings, setting traps at the rear to make an approach by the woods untenable. Because of the roaring wind, the clashing of treetops, Vince had barely caught the sounds of Dietz's demise. But after watching Gerard sink without trace into the quagmire, he feared a different fate had befallen his bowman. Had Simmons also floundered in a watery grave?

Beforehand he'd commanded radio silence, but he was happy to break it now.

'Sound out,' he commanded.

In response, three distinct and individual clicks. He knew that was a lie, because the last thing on Gerard's mind as he choked on mud would be to respond in the affirmative.

'I said sound out. Give me names!'

'Dean Crow,' came a whispered response.

The hairs rose on Vince's neck.

'Tubal Cain,' the voice whispered again.

Ice water ran through Vince.

'The Harvestman,' Martin Maxwell concluded.

Vince didn't respond to the taunting litany of pseudonyms used in the past by his quarry. He was more concerned that Maxwell had replied on one of their radios on the assigned channel: he must've taken it from one of his other men; he certainly hadn't gotten his hands on Gerard's radio. Vince was certain that Dietz was dead somewhere back there in the woods, because the only sign of movement now was by Simmons, whom, swaddled in his Ghillie suit, he'd just spotted approaching the cabin from the west. His rifle was in the high-ready position as he swept the cabin through his IR scope.

'Simmons respond,' Vince snapped curtly into his throat mike.

Simmons raised his fingers, tapping at his earpiece, then made a cutting motion back and forth across his throat, signifying he couldn't speak.

I might look like a dumb hick, Vince thought, *but you don't fool me,* you son of a bitch!

Ten yards separated them: an easy shot with a rifle, not so with a handgun in this storm. But Vince raised the Beretta, caressing the trigger.

Simmons — nay, the Harvestman in Simmons' garb — returned fire, but the blistering rounds snapping through the Ghillie suit caused him to drop low, so his rifle shot went high. Vince hurtled for the cabin, shouldering open the front door without halting. Maxwell fired again, and a bullet punched through a window shutter and struck the inner wall. Vince planted his feet, and laid down three rapid shots in response. Immediately he moved, staying low as he raced through the living room and took shelter in the doorway to a bedroom, the thick doorposts offering a modicum of protection from the rifle rounds.

'Hey inside,' came the Harvestman's voice. It was a rasp, courtesy of an older wound to his throat. 'I gave you my names, how's about you return the favour…so I know who I'm about to kill.'

'Come inside, asshole. See who kills who.'

'You do understand you just walked into another trap, right?' The Harvestman had shifted position. 'I've got the cabin rigged to blow, on the same remote system I used a few minutes ago to switch the lights off and on.'

'Bullshit,' Vince snapped. He too moved, retreating across the living room towards the entrance once more. He fired through the window shutter as he moved, but had no hope of hitting his target. 'Besides,' he said, 'you aren't going to blow the shit outta this place…not while your trophies are still inside.'

'Who says they're inside? Maybe I moved them before your guys settled into their hides. Y'know, somebody should've warned them to observe the local wildlife. See, it struck me when the birds stopped feeding on those berries out there that something was spooking them. Didn't take long to identify where your guys were hiding, or where your other guy would move in. Damn, I've waited a full three days, anticipating meeting *you* in particular, but I have to say, I'm disappointed.'

'You were expecting somebody else?'

'You're not the first Arrowsake killer to try to finish me.'

'Yeah, well, *that* guy's otherwise engaged.'

'Shame. Would've been a happy reunion for me. Not so him when I stripped every inch of bones from his stinking carcass.'

'See, that's never gonna happen now, Maxwell. You might think you have me pinned down, but only one of us is gonna walk away from here today. Guess who that's gonna be.' Vince snorted. 'I'll give you a clue: not you.'

Vince swept the corners of the cabin with his gaze, trying to spot an explosive charge, but if there was a bomb he couldn't see it: unsurprising really. He believed the Harvestman was bluffing, because there'd be little left to reap of his bones if an explosion eviscerated him. However, he sure as shit wasn't sticking around to test his theory. He lurched towards the bedroom, firing the Beretta, stomping as he charged to draw fire. Immediately he dropped, spun and was up again as high-powered rounds punched through the walls. He almost dived out of the door, rolling and coming to a knee in one smooth motion, just as the edge of a Ghillie suit wafted around the near corner. He drilled the dark shape with three bullets, each at centre mass.

The Ghillie continued wafting, caught on the blustery wind.

'Sneaky son of a bitch!' While they'd been stalling, each trying to locate the other's position,

Maxwell had doffed his camouflage and hung it on a post. Ten feet away, Maxwell, mud-coated and grinning, aimed from behind some barrels, rifle stock to his shoulder.

'Drop the pistol,' he said.

Vince stood, without lowering his Beretta a hairsbreadth.

'Drop the gun,' Maxwell repeated, 'or I'll shoot you in the gut, then sit things out til you rot from the inside out.'

'If I drop my pistol, you'll shoot me anyway.'

'Surely you studied me before hunting me down?' said Maxwell. 'Call me old fashioned, but I do possess a set of morals, one of them being a sense of fair play. Shooting things out with you was never my first choice.'

'So whaddaya suggest?'

'Well, let's see; if you drop the gun, I'll extend to you what I'd've been denied if things had gone your way. I'll give you a fighting chance.'

'Why?'

'Why not? It's been boring for months while I've been recuperating. I think its time I got back in the game, and you give me an opportunity to test if I'm ready for it.'

'You'd risk giving up your advantage to test yourself?'

'Hasn't anyone told you...I'm nuts!' Maxwell grinned.

Vince held his breath, deciding. The wind buffeted him, sending his pompadour into disarray.

He lowered his gun.

'Throw it away.'

The Beretta clattered to the ground and Vince toed it aside.

Maxwell rose fully from concealment without lowering his rifle. He was inches shorter than Vince, but then he wasn't wearing cowboy boots. They were of a similar build, but Maxwell was at least fifteen years the young assassin's senior. The advantage was with the rifle, but Maxwell happily slung it aside, drawing from behind his back a Bowie knife. 'What's your poison?' he asked.

Vince drew a sheath knife from his belt. Maxwell eyed the blade — an Ontario MK 3 — nodding in appreciation. It was six-inches of badass cutting edge, serrated along the spine. If it was a good enough weapon for the United States Navy SEALs, it was good enough for most blade aficionados.

Maxwell edged around him, scanning for other weapons. Vince held his blade in a reverse grip. Maxwell jerked his head, indicating a piece of flattened ground on which they could fight. It was where hunters parked their vehicles when at the cabin, hard packed and relatively even, except the storm washing over them had made runnels in the dirt. Discounting the inside of the cabin, it was perhaps the most even ground in miles. Vince moved for it, paralleling Maxwell from about ten feet.

Marty settled his feet, lowered his centre of gravity, the Bowie held obliquely, left hand open and held marginally above the tip. His opponent strutted around him, rooster-like in his cowboy boots and that cock's comb jutting from his forehead. He tossed the blade in his palm, repeatedly reversing his grip

'If you're the type of low rent killer Walter Conrad has to rely on these days, I pity the old fart,' he said. 'At least the other guy he sent was a worthy opponent.'

'Worthy, how? Granted he's kicked your ass twice now,' Vince pointed out, 'but failed to finish you off. Trust me, asshole, I won't make the same mistake.'

'You're an amateur. Think you're going to slice me like a loaf of bread? You're holding your blade as if it still has butter on it.'

'Should slide nicely between your ribs then,' said the Arrowsake assassin as he pivotted swiftly and took a stab at Marty. His announcement was a ploy to draw Marty's guard low, the blade spearing instead for his face. Easily Marty bobbed aside and struck the blade away with the flat of his Bowie. He allowed the ricocheting blade to swipe at his would-be killer's throat. Steel missed flesh by a hair.

The Ontario MK 3 darted for Marty's groin.

Marty sidestepped.

The blade jabbed for his eyes, then at his chest.

Marty ignored both feints, and instead slashed

down at the wrist. The assassin jerked his hand aside at the last moment, but lost a slice of leather from his sleeve. They backed a half step from each other, both wary of over-commitment. Marty grinned, but his opponent wasn't as pleased with their first forays. He dug a toe into the soaked grit, kicked it in Marty's face, and immediately followed the distraction with a deep lunge. Marty ignored the stinging projectiles, but was forced to squint to avoid the blinding dirt. He sucked back his hips, but felt the sting of metal pierce his abdomen: barely a nick, but it galvanised him. He stabbed, and his Bowie pierced the meat of the other man's thigh: a hand grasped his wrist, trapping the blade in flesh. He heard the hiss of pain, the short cough of effort, and caught the assassin's riposte on the back of his left forearm. Both men went chest to chest, each latching onto the other's knife hand. They wrestled as gusts thrashed them with wind-borne debris and beating rain. Their foreheads clashed, and the younger killer wrenched free of the Bowie, lucky that Marty hadn't stabbed so severely that his leg collapsed. Blood pulsed, but not from an artery that'd drain him in minutes. They jostled together, and the younger man got a heel behind Marty's tripping him. He would have fallen if he held onto the killer's wrist, but Marty released it as he danced backwards, finding his balance, even as he dodged further jabs of the Ontario MK 3.

Only once he was clear of the blade's reach did he resettle, and eye the young man. He sucked in a breath as he appraised the wound in his gut. It was skin deep, nothing to worry about: the piercing wound to the other man's leg would prove more troubling. Marty dabbed a finger at the blood sopping his shirt, grimaced.

'You don't look so sure of yourself anymore. Who's the fuckin' amateur now?' the young man crowed as he limped forward.

Fear flashed over Marty's features. He retreated a step.

The young killer lurched in, his injured leg beginning to cramp, and he jabbed again, an inch from where he'd first drawn blood.

'Sucker!' Marty hissed as he buried the Bowie in the man's other thigh. This time he drove the heavy blade with intention, and it cut deep. He twisted the blade, opening the flesh, and blood gushed.

But there were two canny fighters in the duel.

Vince suspected he couldn't beat the wily blades man at his own game, and to survive he must play a dubious hand. He'd forfeited his thigh, to launch a surprise attack of his own. As his knife darted for Maxwell's throat, drawing a parry of his guarding arm, Vince backhanded his left arm, and something unfurled with shocking speed from around his left wrist. It was his weighted guitar string garrotte. It wrapped around Maxwell's neck, even as Vince dropped his knife and caught the weight with expert precision. His leg wounds weren't enough to slow him more than a split second, as he ducked under

Maxwell's left armpit, snapping tight the wire noose around his neck. Crossing his wrists, Vince forced a knee into Maxwell's spine, rearing backwards so that he brought the Harvestman down on top of him. He locked his legs around his opponent's torso, though they were weakened. Together they rolled in the mud, Vince exerting pressure by pulling apart his hands. Maxwell had barely had enough time to gasp before the wire sealed off his windpipe, and bore in to squeeze off the blood flow in his carotid arteries. Even if his head weren't instantly parted from his body, he'd be unconscious in seconds and dead a few more seconds afterwards. Vince roared in victory, even as the storm picked up ferocity.

Maxwell bucked like a fish on a line.

'Die you crazy son of a bitch,' Vince crowed in his ear.

Maxwell continued to fight, and it surprised Vince, because already he should have succumbed. Only as they twisted to one side did he notice the tip of the Bowie jutting alongside Maxwell's ear. The crafty devil had inserted the blade between the garrotte and his neck. It wouldn't ordinarily matter, because the pressure Vince applied would still cut through the neck from the opposite side, except the Bowie's edge was super sharp, and Maxwell was forcing it outward against the guitar string. The wire snapped with a harsh twang! Maxwell reared away, slashing backwards with an elbow at Vince's head. The tip of the elbow caromed off his skull and scarlet flashes swarmed through Vince's brain.

He shook the blow off, but not quickly enough: seated between Vince's legs, Maxwell stabbed down, driving the Bowie clean through his knee and into the dirt. Vince screeched, his legs unfurling from around Maxwell's waist. He was clawing at the handle of the knife even as Maxwell rolled aside and snatched up the Ontario MK 3 dropped earlier in the fight. The Harvestman spun on his knees, raising the fighting knife for a hammering blow at the juncture of Vince's neck and shoulder.

Vince knew he was done.

A rifle cracked, barely heard above the roaring wind.

Blood puffed on the wind, and Maxwell snatched at the wound on his forearm.

The rifle cracked a second time, but already Maxwell was swarming away, and threw himself behind the stack of barrels.

In raw agony, Vince yanked up on the knife, and his skewered knee pulled loose of the ground. He barely had the resolve to pull the blade free of his severed knee joint, and instead fell back, scrambling away on his backside and elbows. A third shot rang out, blasting shards from one of the barrels Maxwell was concealed behind, and Vince glanced where the gunfire originated. Dietz knelt at the far corner of the cabin, ashen and pained. His left arm hung limp, so his bow was useless. It was still a struggle for him to prep, aim and fire a fourth round from the rifle liberated from where Maxwell had dropped it. Maxwell was up and running, and from his trouser pocket he pulled a small device. As he ran, he aimed the small black object behind him, and Vince knew what was coming...

Maxwell hadn't been bluffing!

The cabin erupted in a roaring fireball and shattered logs that eviscerated Dietz in a scarlet instant, and threw Vince down flat on his back, the wind ripped from his lungs as the super-heated pressure wave rode over him. Broken timber rained around him, something solid caroming off his skull and knocking him into a pit of darkness.

Vince had no idea how long he lay unconscious and bleeding, but when he woke it was with startling clarity. It was dawn, and the surrounding bog was alight with the first rays of a new day. The stink was pungent, the smell of decaying vegetation vying for supremacy over that of wet, burnt wood... underlying it all was the coppery waft of his own blood.

He was surprised to be alive. Maxwell had beaten him, and there was a part of his brain that told Vince to expect the worst, but a quick check of his extremities showed them whole, albeit he had been stabbed through the legs three times. His garrotte had been wound around his right leg as a ligature, and had saved him from bleeding to death. His blood had stopped pulsing, but he was weak from its loss. The mud around him was sodden with it, a purplish brown as it mixed with the earth. The pain in his ruined knee was a crimson wash through his mind. He struggled to sit up, woozy from blood loss and the strike to his skull. He blinked around; saw only the smouldering wreckage of the cabin, and a few rags that was all that was left recognisable of Dietz. No, that wasn't true.

A few feet away there was a small plastic box. He'd have ignored it, believing it trash thrown his direction by the explosion, except for the fact it was untouched by mud or fire, and sat perfectly in place. It had been positioned so that he could not miss it.

He dragged his butt around, used his better leg to push off on and reached for the box. It rattled as he picked it up and flipped back the lid. Inside there was a folded note.

A gun was never my first choice of weapon, the Harvestman had scrawled on the paper, *and the use of explosives a last resort. This was not how I hoped our duel would end but your trigger-happy friend forced my hand. I told you I have a set of morals; be they questionable or not, I stand by them. Robert Louis Stephenson once said; "Do not measure success by today's harvest: Measure success by the seeds you plant today." I believe in fair play, and because I was forced down a different route to survival don't think it apt I take my trophy...this time. Be but warned as fresh seeds have been planted: If we meet again, I will reap my due.*

Vince frowned at the message, and the postscript added to it by Martin Maxwell, the Harvestman, then glanced at the rattling object within the box.

In exchange for sparing your life, I ask a small

favour. Please have Walter Conrad return the enclosed to the good doctor Catherine Bryant, with my apologies to her for parting as an ungrateful patient. It shames me now that I terrorised her into thinking I was about to cut out her jaw, and it was still a cruel joke taking her teeth for my collection after she swooned in fear.

Sitting in the bottom of the box was the set of false dentures Maxwell stole from her the day he'd fled Kitty Hawk Bay.

End

ACKNOWLEDGEMENT

This story was originally published by Hetman Publishing in the short story collection Death Toll: Volume 3 End Game in 2019.

Cover image used under a standard content license from WWW.PIXABAY.Com/Reznik89

ABOUT THE AUTHOR

Matt Hilton

Matt Hilton is the author of thirteen high-octane Joe Hunter thrillers, and ten books in the Tess Grey and Po Villere thriller series. He has also published a number of standalone thriller, horror and supernatural novels, including The Girl in the Smoke, Death Pact and Darke. His first book, Dead Men's Dust, was shortlisted for the Intermational Thriller Writers' Debut Book of 2009 Award, and was a Sunday Times and KIndle bestseller.

Printed in Great Britain
by Amazon